Philip
Ridley

The Hooligan's Shampoo

PENGUIN BOOKS

PENGUIN BOOKS

Published by the Penguin Group
Penguin Books Ltd, 27 Wrights Lane, London W8 5TZ, England
Penguin Books USA Inc., 375 Hudson Street, New York, New York 10014, USA
Penguin Books Australia Ltd, Ringwood, Victoria, Australia
Penguin Books Canada Ltd, 10 Alcorn Avenue, Toronto, Ontario, Canada M4V 3B2
Penguin Books (NZ) Ltd, 182–190 Wairau Road, Auckland 10, New Zealand

Penguin Books Ltd, Registered Offices: Harmondsworth, Middlesex, England

First published 1996
1 3 5 7 9 10 8 6 4 2

Copyright © Philip Ridley, 1996
All rights reserved

Set in 12.5/16pt Bembo Monotype
Typeset by Datix International Limited, Bungay, Suffolk
Printed in England by Clays Ltd, St Ives plc

1

WHAT a blue sky! thought Dillon. Not a cloud in sight. And the sea! Smooth as a mirror. My little boat's hardly rocking –

Look! Something's floating towards me! It's very colourful. Looks like one of those bags you get from a supermarket – No! It's a jellyfish! How wonderful! It's sinking now. Lower and lower . . .

The water's so clear. I can see right to the bottom. Look! An octopus! And a whale with a baby whale. And there! A dolphin! Oh, how beautiful –

It's swimming up to me! Higher and higher! Now it's splashing and squeaking beside the boat. What's it trying to say? Splash, squeak, splash, splash –

I know! It wants me to ride on its back.

Yes, Mr Dolphin! Yes! Yes!

I'm climbing over the side of the boat now.

The dolphin is keeping as still as possible for me. Careful! Its back is very slippery. Oh, I'm so excited! I'm going to ride through the ocean on –

'DILLON!'

Darn it! What's Grandpa doing awake? He should be taking his afternoon nap. Ignore him! Nothing must get in the way of –

'DILLON!'

2   Grandpa's shouting is ruining my day-

dream. Look! The sky is turning back into my bedroom ceiling –

'DILLON!'

The sea is a blue carpet!

'DILLON!'

The boat is my bed!

'DILLON!'

And the dolphin – oh, beautiful Mr Dolphin – is nothing but a pillow!

'DILL –'

'ALL RIGHT, GRANDPA!' Dillon called. 'I'LL BE RIGHT WITH YOU!'

2

'WHAT took you so long, Dillon? I've been yelling and yelling! My throat feels like sandpaper!'

'Sorry, Grandp –'

'Don't apologize Dillon. After all, what am I? Nothing but a bedridden old man with hairs on his nose, warts on his chin, and wrinkled from tip to toe. Oh, look at you, Dillon! Hair tangled! T-shirt creased! Jeans crumpled! You've been daydreaming again, haven't you?'

'No, Grandp –'

'Don't deny it, worthless daydreamer! I know you inside out! Your skull's full of all manner of naughty things, that's why I've got to keep you busy. Now, look out of the window and tell me what you see. Strange noises disturbed my nap. What are they?'

'Let's take a look, Grandpa – Aha! Mmm! Ooooo – there's a lorry outside the house opposite. The house that's been empty for so long . . . annnd . . . ooooo! Yes! New people must be moving in, Grandpa!'

'New people! Ugh! Spare me new people! What do they look like, Dillon?'

'I can't see anyone at the moment, Grandpa – Aha! Wait! Mmm – there's a girl!'

'A girl! It's getting worse! Describe her.'

'Ooooo . . . she's got long blonde hair.'

'Ugh!'

'And she's wearing a frilly white dress.'

'Ugh! Ugh!'

'And she's very pretty.'

'Ugh! Ugh! Ugh! Sounds like a hooligan to me!'

'Oh surely not, Grandpa –'

'That's it! Argue with me! Honestly, Dillon, sometimes you're as irritating as an earwig in my underpants! Do something useful and go to the corner shop! I feel a yearning coming on! I need a tangerine to soothe my sore throat. And Dillon . . .'

'Yes, Grandpa?'

'Don't talk to that Hooligan!'

3

TRING! went the bell above the shop door.

'Well, a hungry hello to you, Dillon,' said the shopkeeper.

'And a hungry hello to you, Mr Shopkeeper,' said Dillon.

'What can I get you today? Something for your grandpa no doubt. Well, my shop has something to satisfy every possible yearning. Perhaps a hairy coconut kissed by the tropical sun? Or fine tea from China, scented with bergamot? Or a jar of roasted peppers in olive oil? And here! Something most exotic! Delicious chocolates! Can you guess what's in them – ?'

'I've no idea,' interrupted Dillon. 'All I want is a tangerine.'

'A tangerine!' The shopkeeper looked horrified. 'When I have shelves full of tantalizing tinned goods to tap-dance on your taste-buds!'

'Afraid so.'

The shopkeeper sighed and shook his head despondently. 'Over there! In that box!'

Dillon went to the box and saw a solitary tangerine with a maggot, big as a finger, poking out of it.

'I can't buy this!' Dillon declared. 'It's rotten!'

'Rotten indeed!' gasped the shopkeeper.

'I'll have you know that in some far-flung

places a maggot is considered a delicacy.'

'Well, you should sell it in far-flung places,' said Dillon, walking towards the door. 'Not here!'

'It'll put hairs on your grandpa's nose!'

'He's got hairs on his nose already. A hungry goodbye to you, Mr Shopkeeper.'

Tring!

4

GRANDPA'S going to be really annoyed! thought Dillon. I bet he says. 'I could have trained a monkey to get me a tangerine –'

'Watch where you're going please,' said a voice.

Dillon looked up and saw –

'The Hooligan!' he gasped out loud.

'The what?'

'Oh . . . aha . . . mmm, yes! I'm sorry!' stammered Dillon. 'I didn't mean to be rude. It's just that . . . well, that's what my grandpa called you.'

'The Hooligan?' the girl said, smiling
10 thoughtfully. 'Well, please thank your

grandpa. I like the name. Although, to be honest, you're a ~~bit~~ of a Hooligan too. You nearly knocked me over, storming down the street like that.'

'Ooooo . . . sorry.'

'Apology accepted.' The girl's smile grew wider. 'I'm going to the shop. Do you want to come with me? Perhaps we can be friends.' She held out her hand.

Dillon flinched away. 'I can't! *We* can't! Grandpa told me not to talk to you.' He started backing down the street. 'And don't buy the tangerine. It's got a maggot in it!'

'Sounds delicious!' said the Hooligan.

5

'I COULD have trained a monkey to get me a tangerine!'

'But, Grandp –'

'Oh, don't explain! After all, what am I? Just a tangerineless, bedridden old man with hairs on his nose, warts on his chin, and wrinkled from tip to toe. Honestly, Dillon, you're about as much use as a cockroach in my cocoa! You're not going to cry, are you?'

'No, Grandpa –'

'Don't lie, worthless daydreamer! There's tears in your eyes! Get out before they dribble all over the place. The damp will aggravate my rheumatism.'

   'But –'

   'Go!'

6

DILLON was sitting on his doorstep, drying his eyes, when the Hooligan walked up.

'That Mr Shopkeeper has the strangest things,' she said. 'I didn't even know you could buy locusts dipped in chocolate. You been crying?'

'A little.'

'Why?'

'It's my grandpa. He's always saying nasty things to me! He thinks I'm nothing but a worthless daydreamer.'

'Daydreamer, eh? And what do you day-dream about exactly?'

14   'Ooooo . . . lots of things.'

'Such as?'

'Dolphins.'

'Dolphins!' exclaimed the Hooligan. 'Oh, perr-leeze! How boring! All that squeaking and splashing. What tedious animals!'

'I don't find them tedious at all,' insisted Dillon. 'I find them . . . thrilling!'

'Thrilling! Oh, give me a break. You don't know what thrilling is till you've seen what I've got.'

'G-got? Wh-where?'

'In my room.'

'Wh-what is it?'

'A creature. It lives in a large fish tank. Got sharp teeth so it can eat things like this!' She held a hamburger in the air. 'Raw   15 meat! Fresh from the corner shop! And, when my creature eats, there's so much chomping and splashing and gurgling that I go, "Eeeee!" Come and watch! I bet you'll go "Eeeee!" too.'

'Ooooo . . . I'd love to! Really! But . . . mmm . . . well, my grandpa won't let me.'

The Hooligan stared at Dillon for a while, then said, 'Wait here!' She rushed into her house.

When she returned a few minutes later, she was holding a small silver watering-can. 'A present,' she said. 'To cheer you up.'

'Ooooo . . . thank you,' said Dillon, taking the can. 'But . . . what would I want it for?'

'Who knows?' the Hooligan said, dashing back home. 'All manner of things might need watering one day.'

7

THAT night Dillon lay in bed and looked at the watering-can on his bedside cabinet.

Moonlight glinted off its silver surface.

My first gift! thought Dillon. How good of Hooligan to give it to me! I wish I could be her friend. It would be nice to watch her creature eat hamburgers.

And it would be even nicer to . . . hold her hand.

8

WHAT a blue sky! thought Dillon. Not a cloud in sight. And the sea! Smooth as a mirror. My little boat is hardly rocking –

Look! Something's floating towards me! Looks like a tin bath-tub – No! It's a turtle! Oh, how beautiful –

Now it's blowing bubbles beside the boat. What's it trying to tell me? Bubble, bubble –

I know! It wants me to ride on its back.

Yes, Mr Turtle! Yes! Yes!

I'm climbing over the side of the boat now.

The turtle is keeping as still as possible 19

for me. Careful! Its shell is slippery with sea-
weed. Oh, I'm so excited! I'm going to ride
through the ocean on –

'DILLON!'

Darn it!

9

'WHAT a mess you look, Dillon! Have you been daydreaming again?'

'No, Grandp –'

'That's it! Lie to me! After all, what am I? Just a bedridden old man with hairs on his nose, warts on his chin, and wrinkled from tip to toe. Look out of the window! I can smell something very strange. It's tickling my nose hairs – TISHOO!'

'Let me see, Grandpa – Aha! Mmm! Ooooo – Hooligan is washing her hair. I can see her through the bathroom window. There's soapsuds all over the place. Ooooo . . . so many. They're floating out of the

window and down the street. Oh, they're . . .
remarkable –'

'Don't say "remarkable", Dillon. I've told
you before: there's nothing left remarkable
in the world. And the least remarkable thing
in this unremarkable world is you –
TISHOO!'

'Bless you, Grandp –'

'Don't bless me, Dillon! Just go to the
shop and get me some milk. What with my
sore throat and all this sneezing, I've got a
cold coming on. A cup of warm milk might
help – TISHOO!'

10

TRING!

'Well, a hungry hello to you, Dillon.'

'A hungry hello to you, Mr Shopkeeper.'

'And what has your grandpa a yearning for today? Perhaps some bamboo shoots with water chestnuts, flavoured with aromatic Madras? Or saffron rice with –?'

'Just milk,' interrupted Dillon.

The shopkeeper shook his head. 'I'm wasted in this place,' he sighed. Then indicated a crate in the corner. 'Over there!'

There was only one bottle of milk left and, when Dillon took it from the crate, he saw –

'It's curdled! Grandpa can't drink this!'

''Course he can,' the shopkeeper insisted. 'In some parts of the world milk is only worth drinking when it's tinged with green. Besides, it'll put warts on your grandpa's chin.'

'He's got warts on his chin already.'

'But –'

Tring!

11

GRANDPA'S going to be even more annoyed now! thought Dillon. I bet he says,
'You haven't got the sense God gave
lettuce –'

'Watch it!'

Dillon looked up and saw –

'Hooligan! Ooooo . . . I'm sorry. Did I
nearly walk into you again?'

'You most certainly did,' said the Hooligan. 'But don't worry. I'm getting used to
it.' She smiled and fluttered her eyelashes.
'I'm getting another hamburger. Want to
come with me?'

'I'd like to but . . . ooooo –'

'Oh, that's right! Your grandpa! I forgot! I must say your grandpa sounds as tedious as your dolphins –'

'I like turtles too!'

'Turtles! Oh, perr-leeze! They're even worse. Nothing but a shell with a head so small it's hardly worth having! Might as well daydream about dustbin lids.' She started walking towards the shop.

'Don't buy the milk,' Dillon called after her. 'It's sour and clotted!'

'Sounds scrumptious!'

12

'YOU haven't got the sense God gave lettuce!'

'But, Grandp –'

'Oh, don't explain! After all, what am I but a tangerineless, milkless, bedridden old man. You're not crying again, are you?'

'No, Grandp –'

'Liar! Look at those tears! Damp is the last thing my cold needs. Just like you! No consideration – TISHOO!'

'Bless you.'

'Get out!'

13

As Dillon sat on the doorstep drying his eyes, he heard strange noises coming from the Hooligan's house –

Chomp! Chomp!

Splash! Splash!

Gurgle! Gurgle!

'Eeeeeeeeee!'

Hooligan's feeding her creature! he thought. If only I could see it! I bet its sharp teeth make mincemeat of that hamburger –

'Oh, perr-leeze! Do stop crying.'

'Ooooo . . . hello, Hooligan! I didn't hear you walk up.'

'No wonder! You were too busy

snivelling!'

'Don't be nasty.'

'I'm being honest, not nasty! And just to prove it – here! Another present for you.'

'Wh-what is it?'

'A bag of earth!'

'A bag of earth! But what would I want a bag of earth for?'

'Who knows?' said the Hooligan, plopping the bag in Dillon's lap. 'All manner of things might need planting one day.'

'TISHOO!'

'Oh, perr-leeze!' gasped the Hooligan. 'What a deafening sneeze!'

'It's Grandpa! He says your shampoo irritates his nose hairs! But . . . well, I think your hair smells lovely.'

29

The Hooligan smiled and walked back home.

'Thank you for the earth,' Dillon called after her.

14

THAT night Dillon lay in bed and looked at the bag of earth on his bedside cabinet.

My second gift! he thought. How good of Hooligan to –

'Zzzzz.'

Oh, Grandpa's snoring is disturbing me. I want to think of Hooligan! Not listen to him!

'Zzzzz.'

The way she says 'Perr-leeze'.

'Zzzzz.'

The smell of her hair.

'Zzzzz.'

Holding her hand . . .

15

WHAT a blue sky! thought Dillon. Not a cloud in sight! And the sea! Smooth as a mirror. My little boat is –

'TISHOO!'

– hardly rocking.

'TISHOO!'

Darn it! Grandpa's sneezing will wake him up. Then he'll –

'DILLON!'

Knew it!

16

'LOOK how ill I am, Dillon! Sore throat! Sneezing! And now I'm shivering so much my dentures are rattling. But are you bothered? No! You're in your room daydreaming!'

'I'm not, Grandp –'

'Don't deny it! Just buy me a blanket. I have a yearning to keep warm.'

17

TRING!

'Well, a hungry –'

'A blanket.'

'My! You're in a bad mood! Why don't you buy some of these delicious chocolates. Have you guessed what's in them yet –'

'I don't care! Just give me a blanket.'

'The chocolates are easier to swallow.'

'Spare me the jokes.'

The shopkeeper sighed and pointed to a shelf. 'Over there! One left, I think.'

'Thank you! Oh, look at the state of it! Full of holes.'

'You're exaggerating, surely!'

'No, I'm not! In fact, it's more holes with a blanket than a blanket with holes. I can't buy this!'

'But –'

'Chew a locust!'

Tring!

GRANDPA'S going to be more annoyed than ever now! thought Dillon. I bet he says 'You're two tokens short of a toaster –'

'Watch it! You nearly walked into me again –'

'Then *you* watch where *you're* going, Hooligan!'

'My! Who rattled *your* cage?'

'Everyone!'

'Why don't you come with me to buy a –'

'Hamburger! For your creature! I know! Next you'll be asking me to come and watch your creature! Well, I can't! You know that! So stop asking!'

   'I only want to be friends –'

   'Oh, go buy a burger!'

   'But –'

   'Bye!'

19

'YOU'RE two tokens short of a toaster!'
  'Sob!'
  'Stop crying, Dillon.'
  'Sob!'
  'Oh, get out!'

20

DILLON sat on the doorstep still going –

'Sob!'

And heard –

Chomp!

Splash!

Gurgle!

'Eeeee!'

Who wants to see Hooligan's creature anyway? I don't! Who cares if it goes chomp? I don't! Who cares if it makes Hooligan go 'Eeeee!'? I don't! I don't care about anything –

'Don't cry,' said the Hooligan, tapping Dillon's shoulder.

'Ooooo – you made me jump! And if you've come over here to say anything nasty, then you can just go straight back home –'

'I haven't come to say anything nasty. I've come to give you yet another present.' The Hooligan handed him a small bottle of bright-pink liquid. 'It's my shampoo,' she said. Then, noticing Dillon's confused look, continued, 'Well, you *did* say you liked the smell. And your hair *is* a bit of a mess. All tangled with daydreams, I shouldn't wonder. So I thought . . . well, the shampoo might do some untangling.'

'You're always giving me presents. Why?'

'Well . . . to be honest. I'm finding it hard to enjoy my creature, knowing you're sad. I know it sounds wishy-washy! But I can't help it!'

And with that, the Hooligan dashed back into her house.

21

THAT night Dillon lay in bed and waited for his grandpa to fall asleep.

On his bedside cabinet was the silver watering-can.

And the bag of earth.

And the bottle of shampoo.

'Zzzzz!'

At last! thought Dillon.

He grabbed the shampoo and dashed to the bathroom.

22

I FEEL stupid doing this! thought Dillon, sticking his head under the tap. What can possibly happen just by washing my hair in a different shampoo? Well, that's my hair wet. Where's the bottle?

Here it is!

Unscrew the lid!

Pour shampoo on my head!

Rub it in!

It smells very strong. Much stronger than when it made Grandpa's nose hairs itch yesterday. But, then again, now it's on my head, not across the street.

Difficult to describe the smell.

Like all the best things from far away places mixed together.

Aha! Some soap's in my eyes! Ooooo!

Best rinse them with water . . .

That's better.

Oh, look! The bathroom's full of bubbles. Like being in a washing-machine.

Now . . . rinse my hair.

That's it!

Hair all clean and free of tangles.

But . . . that's all!

Nothing else is happening!

Oh, well . . . back to bed.

23

As Dillon lay in bed the smell of the shampoo hovered round him.

He felt very peaceful and calm.

And, that night, he dreamed . . .

24

I'm in a desert! Nothing but sand everywhere. And the sun's very hot! Hotter than I've ever felt it. Like being in an oven.

Phew! I'm sweating! It's trickling down my face. And my back.

I'm so thirsty.

But there's nothing to drink! Just sand and sand and –

Wait! What's that?

Something on the sand up ahead. It's the size of a billiard ball and –

It's a tangerine!

Perfect! I can drink its juice.

Mmm . . . delicious. That's quenched my

thirst. I only hope it doesn't put hairs on my nose.

Ahhh! The sun is really burning my skin. Now I know what it feels like to be a slice of bread in a toaster.

I wish I had something to soothe the burning –

Wait! What's that?

A bottle of something in the sand up ahead. It looks like a milk bottle –

That's because it is! Milk! Perfect! I can soothe my skin with it.

Mmm . . . that feels better. I only hope it doesn't put warts on my chin.

Ooooo! The sun's setting now! Getting colder by the second.

Look! Now it's night! I'm freezing.   47

I wish I had something to keep me warm —

Wait! What's this?

A blanket! Perfect! I'll wrap it round me.

Mmm . . . I'm as snug as a bug in a rug. I only hope it doesn't wrinkle me from tip to toe —

Wait! What's that?

Something in the sand —

It's a flower!

A large white bloom with multicoloured specks.

It's so beautiful!

Let's pick the —

25

'– FLOWER!' said Dillon, waking.

It was morning now and sunlight streamed through the window.

The clock on the bedside cabinet told Dillon that he had overslept by almost two hours.

I've never done that before! he thought with surprise.

And then he saw something even more surprising.

Something that made him gasp out loud.

Because in his hand was the flower.

26

It can't be! thought Dillon. How can I dream a flower, then still have it when I'm awake? It's just not possible –

'DILLON – TISHOO!'

Dillon stared at the flower.

Then at the silver watering-can.

Then the bag of earth.

'DILLON – TISHOO!'

And suddenly he knew what to do.

'WHERE have you been, Dillon? I've been calling and calling! My sore throat is red raw now! And my sneezing has given me a headache. And my shivering's rattled the dentures from my head – What are you doing?'

'Pouring this bag of earth on to your bed, Grandpa.'

'Why?'

'I'm not sure yet.'

'Wh–what are you doing now?'

'Planting this flower in the earth, Grandpa.'

'Why?'

'I'm not sure yet.'

'Wh-wh-what are you doing now?'

'Watering the flower with this silver watering-can.'

'Why?'

'I'm not sure yet.'

'B-b-but look at the state of my bed, Dillon. It's earthy and wet with a flower sticking out of it! Not even a monkey would be this stupid! Even a lettuce leaf would have more sense. You must be more tokens short of a toaster than I ever realized –'

'SHUT UP, GRANDPA!' Dillon suddenly yelled. 'YOU'RE A SELFISH OLD MAN WHO HAS NO REASON TO BE BEDRIDDEN AT ALL!'

52   And that's when it happened!

28

THE flower on the bed sprouted another flower.

Then another flower.

Then another.

Another!

'Wh-what's happening, Dillon?'

'Something remarkable.'

Now stalks and leaves were sprouting.

And on every stalk were more flowers.

And those flowers sprouted more stalks.

And those stalks more flowers.

And more.

More!

Their scent filled the room.

And that's when the stalks lifted the bed into the air . . .

29

'Ahhhhh!' cried Grandpa, falling out of the bed.

He landed with a thump on the floor.

The floor that was now covered with –

Yellow flowers!

Blue flowers!

Pink flowers!

And now the flowers were spilling out of the room.

Going into the hallway.

Up walls!

Down stairs!

Across ceilings!

Filling the house!

'Scary!' gasped Grandpa. Then sniffed a nearby bloom. 'And beautiful!'

30

WHEN the flowers had filled the house they stopped growing.

Grandpa got to his feet and looked round.

Slowly, he stepped out into the hall.

'Orchids,' Grandpa said, his eyes full of wonder. 'That's what the flowers are called. I used to grow them when I was a gardener. Years ago. Before you were born! Oh . . . look at them!' His voice was softer and gentler than Dillon had ever heard it. 'They need so much looking after. You have to tend to their every whim day and night.' He grinned very wide. 'What fun!'

'Can I go out and play with Hooligan now, Grandpa?' asked Dillon.

'Of course, Dillon,' replied Grandpa, kissing the top of his grandson's head. 'And I'm sorry if I've been a grumpy old so-and-so for most of your life. Things will change from now on. I promise you!' Another kiss. 'You go and enjoy yourself, while I tend my favourite flowers in all the world!'

31

KNOCK! Knock!

The Hooligan opened the door.

'You're just in time,' she said to Dillon, holding a hamburger in the air. 'Feeding time!'

She led him to her room.

A large fish-tank was in the corner.

In the tank was a multicoloured fish with sharp teeth.

'What is it?' asked Dillon.

'A piranha,' she told him. 'Watch!'

The Hooligan dropped the hamburger into the water.

The piranha darted at the raw meat. 59

Sharp teeth flashed.

Bubbles erupted!

Chomp!

Gurgle!

Slurp!

'Eeèee!' went the Hooligan, holding Dillon's hand.

'Eeeee!' went Dillon, holding the Hooligan's hand.

PENGUIN CHILDREN'S 60s